To Esther, this is for you with
lots of love x — Juliet Clare Bell

For Mia-Rose, the peskiest little
princess I know — Laura-Kate Chapman

the Kite Princess

Written by Juliet Clare Bell
Illustrated by Laura-Kate Chapman
Narrated by Imelda Staunton

Barefoot Books
step inside a story

There once was a princess called Cinnamon Stitch.
Her parents were stuffy and terribly rich.

They liked to parade her around their fine land,
With Cinnamon looking exceedingly grand.

They thought if they bought her the best clothes and pearls,
Their daughter would be the most happy of girls.
They gave her fine ribbons and dresses galore…
Then called for the seamstress, who made her some more.

'And now,' said the queen, 'let us practise *deportment*.'

'I *know* how to walk! Are you sure it's important?

Why can't I just read? It's a book, not a hat!'

'You must learn to *glide*, all princesses know that.'

But Cinnamon longed to be wild and free...

So she t u g g ed,

P u l l e d

and wriggled,

and shouted,

'Yippee!'

She cartwheeled in puddles and clambered up trees,
And danced with some cats that were covered in fleas.

She swam in the lake and the weeds in her hair
Made her slimy and grimy, but she didn't care.

A boy at the gates whispered, 'Join us and play.'
But the guards caught her up and they whisked her away...

'Princesses don't cartwheel or clamber up trees!'

'They don't get all slimy and never get fleas!'

'They sing and they sew;
they don't do as they please!'

A sent-to-bed Cinnamon, frowning and yawning,
Then had an idea, which came quite without warning.
Could this really work? She would try the next morning...

As soon as the sun rose, she started to sew.

The queen said so proudly, 'She's changed, don't you know!
We think it's a dress…Yes! She's *such* a delight.
Our beautiful girl. What a marvellous sight!'
(If only they'd known, they'd have had such
a fright!)

Young Cinnamon sewed every day at her chair,
And dreamt every night of the wind in her hair.

She stitched as she stared at the endless blue sky.

She stitched as she gazed at the birds gliding by.

At last she was ready...

and floated up high.

A small girl glanced up. 'Look! The princess is flying!'
　　Her mother said, 'Nonsense! You must stop this lying!'
But somebody heard her and he had a look,
　　Told *his* friends and neighbours and that's all it took
For the news to spread quickly: the sight was so curious.
　　The maid gasped, 'The king and the queen will be furious!'

Guards said to the servants, 'We must get that kite...'
But stood there, entranced by the breathtaking sight.

'What's this?' boomed the queen. 'Why the crowd?
                                    Where's our daughter?'
She looked up, and fainted. The king called out, 'Water!'

Then as she recovered, the mystified queen
    Was sure she heard singing, so sweet and serene.
'Yes, I heard it, too!' said the king to his wife.
    'But she's never sung in the whole of her life…'

'Yippee!'

'My queen,' he went on, 'how she longs to be free!'
They looked at each other and cried, 'So do we!'
And down through the sky came a far-off 'Yippee!'

They summoned the seamstress and set her to sew.
'Two kites, if you please. We're just raring to go!'

They're all happy now and they're less stuffy too.
With Cinnamon's stitching, their world grew and grew.

With Cinnamon's stitching, they took off and flew.

Make Your Own Kite!

What you will need:

- Thin green garden canes (you'll need six per kite and a few spares may be useful.)
- Small craft saw
- Sticky tape
- A big sheet of tissue paper, and other sheets in different colours for decoration
- Felt-tip pen
- PVA glue
- Glitter, feathers, leaves and/or sequins for decoration
- String
- Coloured ribbon

Making your kite

Ask an adult to help you cut the garden canes and hold the joints while you tape them together.

1. Use one cane as the central spine of the kite. Cut four canes to create two longer and two shorter pieces to make the edges of the kite. Then cut one for the crossbar.

2. Join the canes with sticky tape to create the frame. Make the joints strong by placing one cane on top of another and wrapping the tape around the canes tightly.

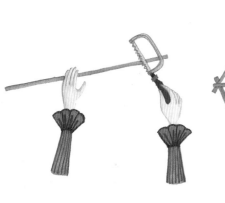

3. Draw around the kite frame on the tissue paper with a felt-tip pen, leaving roughly ten centimetres of space around the kite to wrap around the frame. Cut out this kite shape.

4. Fold the tissue paper over the edge of the kite frame and use the glue to stick it down. It doesn't matter how messy it looks. Let the glue dry.

5. Make your kite special. Cut out shapes of different coloured tissue paper and stick them on with glue. Or stick on glitter, feathers, leaves or sequins. Use your imagination!

6. Once the glue is dry, tie a long string to the base of your kite to create the tail. Decorate the tail by tying short lengths of ribbon along the string.

7. Tie a piece of string at two places along the crossbar. Tie another piece along the spine. Tie them together where they meet in the middle with one end of a really long piece of string. This will be the string you hold when you fly the kite.

Have some fun with your kite!

Barefoot Books
294 Banbury Road
Oxford, OX2 7ED

First published in Great Britain by Barefoot Books, Ltd in 2012
The hardback edition with story CD first published in 2012
The paperback edition with story CD first published in 2012

Graphic design by Ryan Scheife, Mayfly Design, Minneapolis, MN
Reproduction by B & P International, Hong Kong
Printed in China on 100% acid-free paper
This book was typeset in Grandma, LD Honeydukes, Verner and Janda Curlygirl
The illustrations were prepared using watercolours, felt tips, pencil crayons, collage, and pencil.
All elements were created by hand and then scanned in and laid out using Photoshop.

Hardback ISBN 978-1-84686-802-3
Paperback ISBN 978-1-84686-829-0

British Cataloguing-in-Publication Data:
a catalogue record for this book is available from the British Library

1 3 5 7 9 8 6 4 2

Barefoot Books
Step inside a story

At Barefoot Books, we celebrate art and story that opens the hearts
and minds of children from all walks of life, focusing on themes that
encourage independence of spirit, enthusiasm for learning and respect
for the world's diversity. The welfare of our children is dependent on
the welfare of the planet, so we source paper from sustainably managed
forests and constantly strive to reduce our environmental impact.
Playful, beautiful and created to last a lifetime, our products combine
the best of the present with the best of the past to educate our
children as the caretakers of tomorrow.

www.barefootbooks.com

Juliet Clare Bell worked on *The Kite Princess* in short
sessions whenever her young children dozed off. She previously
worked in research as a developmental psychologist, specialising
in early years. She now writes, visits schools and runs events for
the Society of Children's Book Writers and Illustrators.
She lives in Birmingham with her family.
www.julietclarebell.com

Laura-Kate Chapman is a Liverpool-based freelance
illustrator. She enjoys creating unusual and convincing characters
and weaving intricate and eccentric patterns into her work. She
says, 'My aim is to create a visual world that gives the mundane
a more magical feel, and above all else I want my illustrations
to make people smile.'
www.laura-katedraws.co.uk

Imelda Staunton has acted with both the RSC and the National
Theatre, winning two Olivier awards. Her many screen roles
include the title role in *Vera Drake*, which won her a BAFTA
and Oscar nomination, and Professor Umbridge in two Harry
Potter films. Imelda was awarded an OBE for services to drama
in 2006.